Billie B Brown

www.BillieBBrown.com

The Missing Tooth
published in 2012 by
Hardie Grant Egmont
Ground Floor, Building 1, 658 Church Street
Richmond, Victoria 3121, Australia
www.hardiegrantegmont.com.au

A CiP record for this title is available from the National Library of Australia

Text copyright © 2012 Sally Rippin
Illustration copyright © 2012 Aki Fukuoka
Logo and design copyright © 2012 Hardie Grant Egmont

Design and typeset by Stephanie Spartels

Printed in China by Everbest Printing Co.

Billie B Brown

The Missing Tooth

By Sally Rippin

Illustrated by Aki Fukuoka

hardie grant EGMONT

Chapter One

Billie B Brown has two messy pigtails, fifteen freckles and one wobbly tooth. Do you know what the B in Billie B Brown stands for?

Bother.

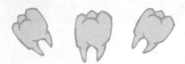

Every morning this
week, Billie B Brown
has stood in front of
the mirror and wiggled
and jiggled her wobbly
tooth. But it is no use.
The tooth is stuck.
What a bother!

Fifteen freckles

Two messy pigtails

One wobbly tooth

3

'Billie, stop fiddling with your tooth,' Billie's mum says. 'It will come out when it's ready. Hurry and brush your teeth or you'll be late for school.'

Billie's mum is a bit **grumpy** today. Noah has been crying a lot in the night, so she is very tired.

Noah's cheeks are bright red and he is very **dribbly**. Billie's mum says he is teething.

Billie brushes her teeth carefully. Billie's dad pokes his head into the bathroom.

'I can pull out your tooth for you,' he jokes.

6

'I just have to tie one end of a string around your tooth and the other end to the doorknob. Then, **slam!** Out pops the tooth!'

'No way!' says Billie, spitting toothpaste into the sink. 'That will hurt!'

Billie walks to school with her dad and her best friend, Jack.

On the way, she starts
wiggling the wobbly
tooth again.

'How about eating an
apple?' Jack suggests.
'That's how I lost one
of mine.'

Billie shakes her head.
'That might hurt,'
she says.

8

She pushes her hands
down into her pockets to
stop her fingers creeping
up to her mouth.

At school, Billie's class
is learning about teeth.
They learn that an elephant
has big pointy teeth called
tusks. Crocodiles have
70 teeth and sharks have
three sets of teeth. Even
slugs have teeth!

Ms Walton asks how
many people in the class
have lost a tooth.

11

Everyone puts up their hand – except Billie.

Billie frowns and looks down at her desk.

Hurry up, tooth! she thinks.

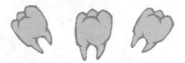

Chapter Two

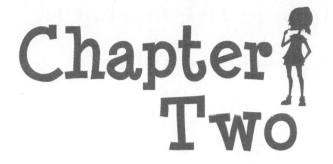

At playtime, Billie
and Jack play chasey
with some other kids in
their class. First Jack is It.
He chases Billie around
the playground.

Billie is very fast but Jack traps her near the drink taps. 'Billie's It!' he shouts.

Billie decides she is going to catch Mika next. Mika is a fast runner too. But not as fast as Billie. Billie runs and runs and runs and…Oh no! Billie trips over. She falls down hard onto the concrete.

Even though she stuck
out her hands, Billie
still bangs her chin on
the ground. She sits up
and **howls**.

Billie's hands are grazed, her knees are grazed – even her chin is grazed. She feels **sore** all over. Poor Billie!

Jack rushes over. Mika, Ella and Tracey rush over too. Hot tears stream down Billie's cheeks. Mika puts her arm around Billie.

'I'll take her to sick bay!'
Ella offers.

'No, I will!' says Tracey.
'It's my turn.'

'You can all come,'
Billie sniffles. 'I need all
of you to help me walk.
My knees hurt SO much.'

Billie's friends help her
stand up.

'Wait!' Jack says. 'Look!'

Billie looks at the ground. There, in the dust, is something very small and white. It's not much bigger than a grain of rice. Can you guess what it is?

'My tooth!' Billie **gasps**.

Billie slips her tongue into the gap between her teeth.

It feels **squishy** and tastes like metal. Billie knows that taste. She gasps again. 'Is there blood?'

Ella peers into Billie's mouth. 'A little bit,' she says.

Tracey scrunches up her face like she has swallowed something sour.

Billie begins to feel **worried**.

'It's fine,' says Jack. 'There's hardly any.' He picks up the tiny tooth and hands it to Billie.

Just then Ms Walton
walks over.

'Billie fell over!' Ella shouts.

'Oh my goodness,' says
Ms Walton. 'Look at
your poor knees. And
your chin! We'd better
get you cleaned up.'

'Look!' Billie says.
She shows Ms Walton the
little tooth in her hand.

Ms Walton smiles.
She pulls out a tissue
from her pocket. 'Here,'
she says. 'You don't want
to lose that. Wrap it up
so you can take it home
for the Tooth Fairy.'

Billie grins. The Tooth
Fairy! Even though her
knees and hands and
chin hurt, she can't help
feeling **excited**.

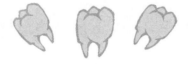

Chapter Three

Billie's dad picks her up after school. Billie is covered in bandaids.

'Oh no, Billie! What happened?' her dad asks.

But Billie is too excited
to bother about all
her injuries.

'I fell over. But look!'
Billie says. Carefully she
unwraps the tissue to
show her dad the tooth.

Billie's dad smiles.
'How exciting,' he says.
'Don't lose it, will you?
Looks like the Tooth
Fairy might be visiting
our house tonight!'

Billie gives a **happy**
little squeal. She wraps
the tooth up in the
tissue again and puts
it in her pocket.

All the way home in the car, her tongue keeps wriggling into the empty space in her mouth.

When they get home, Billie runs into the house to show her mum her tooth. Billie's mum is on the couch feeding Noah. She looks very tired.

'Mum, Mum!' Billie yells.
'Look, look!'

Billie yells so **loudly**
that Noah gets a fright
and starts crying. At first
Billie's mum looks cross.

But then she sees all Billie's bandaids. 'Oh, my poor little soldier! What happened to you?' she says.

'I fell over,' Billie says glumly. 'But look!'
She opens her mouth to show the gap where her tooth had once been.

'Your tooth came out!' says Billie's mum.

She gives Billie a cuddle.
Noah grizzles unhappily.

Billie frowns. 'He's always crying these days,' she says **crossly**.

Billie's mum stands up to rock Noah to sleep.

'It's not his fault,' she sighs. 'He is growing teeth, Billie. They hurt his gums.'

But Billie doesn't want to talk about Noah's teeth. She wants to talk about hers! 'Look,' Billie says. She reaches into her pocket and pulls out the tissue.

She opens it up carefully,
but…the tissue is empty!

'Wait,' says Billie.
She checks her pocket.
There is nothing there.

'Oh no,' she says. She feels
her bottom lip begin to
tremble. 'I can't find it!'

'Maybe it fell out in
the car?' Billie's mum says.

Billie checks the car
all over. But the tooth is
nowhere to be found.

Billie starts to cry. Her knees
hurt, her hands hurt, even
her chin hurts. And now
she has lost her tooth, too!

Chapter Four

That night, Billie's dad
tucks Noah into bed.
Her mum sits on Billie's
bed. Billie still feels very
upset.

'Oh, Billie,' says her mum.

She gives Billie a cuddle.
'Maybe the Tooth Fairy
will still come?'

But Billie shakes her
head sadly. It's no use.
Everyone knows the
Tooth Fairy only comes if
there is a tooth to collect.

Just then Billie has an idea.

A super-dooper idea.

'I know!' she says, wiping her eyes. 'Maybe I can write the Tooth Fairy a note?'

'That's a great idea!' says Billie's mum.

So Billie gets out her sparkly pens and writes a note for the fairy. She even draws a picture.

Dear Tooth Fairy,

I lost my first tooth today.
I fell over at school and
banged my chin and my tooth
came out. But then I lost

my tooth on my way home from school (this is the truth!).
Can you please still leave me some money anyway?
Otherwise my friends won't believe that you came.

From,
Billie

PS If you don't believe me, check my mouth.

PPS I will try to sleep with my mouth open,
but if it's closed, could you come
back in a little while?

PPPS Please don't wake my brother
because he is teething.

Billie tucks the note
under her pillow.
Then her mum gives
her a goodnight kiss.

The next morning, when
Billie wakes up, she sits
up slowly. Her knees and
hands still ache and her
chin feels sore. Billie feels
for her wobbly tooth. Oh,
that's right – it's gone!

Billie suddenly
remembers. The Tooth
Fairy! Did she come?
Billie lifts up her pillow.
There, lying on her bed
sheet, is a shiny gold coin.

'Mum, Dad!' Billie yells. She runs to find her parents. Billie's dad is already awake. He has Noah in his arms.

'Shhh…' he says. 'Your mum is still sleeping. What is it, Billie?'

'The Tooth Fairy came!' Billie whispers excitedly.

'She must have read my note because she left me money!'

'Well, there you are,' says Billie's dad, smiling. 'That's great, Billie! It looks like the Tooth Fairy had a busy night. Look!'

Billie's dad gently opens Noah's mouth.

Billie peers inside. And there, on his bottom gum, is a shiny white tooth, as small as a grain of rice.

Billie B Brown
The Bad Butterfly
By Sally Rippin
1

Billie B Brown
The Soccer Star
By Sally Rippin
2

Billie B Brown
The Second-best Friend
By Sally Rippin
3

Billie B Brown
The Midnight Feast
By Sally Rippin
4

Billie B Brown
The Beautiful Haircut
By Sally Rippin
5

Billie B Brown
The Extra-special Helper
By Sally Rippin
6

Billie B Brown
The Secret Message
By Sally Rippin
7

Billie B Brown
The Big Sister
By Sally Rippin
8

Billie B Brown
The Birthday Mix-up
By Sally Rippin
9

Billie B Brown
The Little Lie
By Sally Rippin
10

Billie B Brown
The Best Project
By Sally Rippin
11

Billie B Brown
The Spotty Holiday
By Sally Rippin
12

Billie B Brown
The Cutest Pet Ever
By Sally Rippin
13

Billie B Brown
The Pocket Money Blues
By Sally Rippin
14

Billie B Brown
The Copycat Kid
By Sally Rippin
15

Billie B Brown
The Deep End
By Sally Rippin
16

Billie B Brown
The Night Fright
By Sally Rippin
17

Billie B Brown
The Missing Tooth
By Sally Rippin
18

Billie B Brown
The Big Bully
By Sally Rippin
19

Billie B Brown
The Perfect Present
By Sally Rippin
★